USHA
the
mouse-maiden

USHA

the
mouse-maiden

Retold and illustrated by
MEHLLI GOBHAI

Hawthorn Books, Inc.
Publishers   New York

To Bernice

More than a thousand years ago, in India, there was a very old sage named Yajnavalkya.

He and his wife lived in a cool, thick forest through which flowed the sacred river Ganges. One day, at dawn, he went to the water's edge to pray.

The piercing cry of a bird disturbed his prayers.

He looked up and saw an angry hawk circling above him.

Just then something soft and warm fell into his hand. The hawk had dropped its prey.

The sage slowly opened his hand. Crouching in the hollow of his palm was a baby mouse. Its tiny, soft body was shaking with terror.

The old man carefully placed the frightened creature on a banyan leaf and finished his prayers. Then, through his magic powers, he changed the little mouse into a beautiful baby girl.

He carried the child home to his wife.

"Take her, my dear wife," he said. "She is a gift from the Gods."

His wife took the warm, glowing child into her arms. She was filled with a great happiness. Here, at last a child of her own—the answer to all her prayers.

They named the little girl Usha, after the dawn, and loved her like a daughter.

The years went happily by, and soon Usha bloomed into a radiant young woman.

As she wandered through the forest, the animals walked with her, spellbound by her beauty and grace.

One morning the wife said,

"I think it is time for us to find a husband for our daughter."

"She shall have the most splendid of all husbands," said the old man. "I shall give her in marriage to the Sun!"

And so the holy man summoned the Sun. The Sun God came blazing down in all his golden splendour, scorching the leaves of the forest and burning the grass under him.

But the young girl turned away and cried,

"I cannot even look at him, my Father. He is too dazzling and hot."

Then the wife said,

"Do not fret, my child. Your father will find you a husband even greater than the Sun."

"O Sun, is there one greater than you?" asked the old man, and the Sun replied,

"The Cloud is greater, for he can cover me and steal my light."

Then the holy man summoned the Cloud.

The Cloud God descended in a darkening sky, and the animals of the forest fled before him.

"Will you take the Cloud for your husband?" the old man asked his daughter.

"Oh no, my Father," said Usha. "He is too dark and forbidding for me."

"Is there one greater than you, O Cloud?" asked the hermit.

"The Wind," replied the Cloud, "for with one strong gust he can drive me where it pleases him."

So the old man summoned the Wind to him. The Wind God came roaring through the great forest. Even the tallest and the strongest trees bent and swayed in his path.

"He is too nervous and shifty!" cried Usha.

"Who is greater than you, O Wind?" asked the old man.

"The Mountain," replied the Wind, "for he alone can stand in my way and stop me."

Then the old man summoned the Mountain, and the ground shook as the Mountain answered with a thousand echoes.

"I have at last found the greatest one of all, my child," said the old man to his daughter.

"Please do not force me to marry him, my Father," Usha cried. "How could I live with one so rough and craggy?"

"Who can be greater than you, O Mountain?" cried the old man in despair, and the echoes answered, "None could be greater than he who nibbles at the Mountain."

Just then, a tiny mouse scampered out of the thick forest. He ran straight to Usha and sat at her feet.

His shiny coat was soft, burnished gold, and his twitching nose was as pink as the sky at dawn.

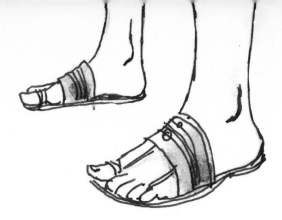

At the sight of this beautiful creature, a thrill went through the young maiden, and her heart was filled with love for the little mouse. She fell on her knees and cried out:

"Dear Father, please change me into a mouse. I will be truly happy only if I can marry him and no other."

Then, the old man knew what he must do. Using his magic powers once more, he changed his daughter back into a mouse.

For a moment Usha stood quietly in front of the holy man, her eyes shining with love and happiness.

Then she turned to the little mouse waiting beside her, and together they ran swiftly into the cool, thick forest.

ABOUT THE STORY

The Mouse-Maiden was probably first told in India several thousand years ago. Later, about 200 B.C., it was written in Sanskrit, the classical Indian language.

This story is a part of the Panchatantra (meaning "five books"), which contains eighty-four *niti* or moral tales. The *Panchatantra* was originally written by a holy man, to educate a wise rajah's three foolish sons.

English- and German-language versions of the *Panchatantra* were among the first books to be printed from movable type in the fifteenth century, and other translations continue to be popular.

ABOUT THE AUTHOR/ARTIST

Mehlli Gobhai is a native of Bombay, India. He received his B.A. in economics and political science and attended law school there before going to the Royal College of Art in London.

Mr. Gobhai has worked as an art director in the Bombay, London, and New York offices of a major advertising firm. He now lives in a New York City apartment, which he shares with an English bulldog and two Siamese cats, dividing his time between painting and writing.